Curtain Call

Also by Jennifer L. Holm & Matthew Holm

Sunny Side Up

Swing It, Sunny

The Babymouse series

The Squish series

My First Comics series

Also by Jennifer L. Holm

Boston Jane: An Adventure

Boston Jane: Wilderness Days

Boston Jane: The Claim

The Creek

The Fourteenth Goldfish

The Third Mushroom

Middle School Is Worse Than Meatloaf

Eighth Grade Is Making Me Sick

Our Only May Amelia

The Trouble with May Amelia

Penny from Heaven

Turtle in Paradise

Full of Beans

Also by Matthew Holm
(with Jonathan Follett)

Marvin and the Moths

Random House 🏠 New York

JENNIFER L. HOLM & MATTHEW HOLM

BABYMOUSE
TALES FROM THE LOCKER

Curtain Call

Copyright © 2020 by Jennifer Holm and Matthew Holm

All rights reserved. Published in the United States by Random House Children's Books, a division of Penguin Random House LLC, New York.

Random House and the colophon are registered trademarks of Penguin Random House LLC.

Visit us on the Web! rhcbooks.com

Educators and librarians, for a variety of teaching tools, visit us at RHTeachersLibrarians.com

Library of Congress Cataloging-in-Publication Data
Names: Holm, Jennifer L., author. | Holm, Matthew, author, illustrator.
Title: Curtain call / Jennifer L. Holm and Matthew Holm.
Description: First edition. | New York : Random House, [2020]
Series: Babymouse. Tales from the locker; 4
Summary: "Babymouse tries out for the middle school play, but instead of landing the lead role, she gets stuck with playing a clown with one line of dialogue." —Provided by publisher.
Identifiers: LCCN 2019011985 (print) | LCCN 2019016461 (ebook)
ISBN 978-0-593-11936-5 (hardback)
ISBN 978-0-593-11937-2 (glb) | ISBN 978-0-593-11938-9 (ebook)
Subjects: | CYAC: Theater—Fiction. | Middle schools—Fiction.
Schools—Fiction. | Mice—Fiction. | Animals—Fiction. | Humorous stories.
Classification: LCC PZ7.H732226 (ebook)
LCC PZ7.H732226 Cur 2020 (print)

Printed in the United States of America
10 9 8 7 6 5 4 3 2 1
First Edition

For Polo

Contents

Invisible

If I could choose a superpower, I would pick X-ray vision, or super-straight whiskers, or even being good at fractions. I would never, ever pick invisibility. Why? Because that's basically my life right now: being invisible. And let me tell you, it's not all that great!

My best friend, Wilson, says it's all in my head. But I really don't think it is. When I walk down the hallway, people don't even notice me. It's like I'm a ghost.

And it's not like I don't **try** to stand out.

I thought that by dressing like the popular girls, I might get noticed. But even **that** didn't work.

Of course, the one time I **don't** want to get noticed is in class, but that never happens.

I can't tell you how many times people have turned the lights out on me. The gym teacher almost locked me in the gym the other day!

I was so frustrated by not being noticed.
Everywhere I looked, other kids stood out.

Even the custodian was famous now that he was starring on the **Real Custodians of Middle School** TV series!

I thought about this as I waited in the lunch line. I didn't want to stand out for the **wrong** reasons. (No one wants to be the kid who eats the stinky block of blue cheese every day for lunch.)

But how hard was it to get a little attention? I just wanted a teensy-weensy bit of fame. You know, like being featured on a fashion magazine cover or the home page of Tubular.

Hey, I'd even settle for five million likes on social media!

I guess I was still daydreaming when I walked out of the cafeteria, because I wasn't **exactly** looking where I was going. I accidentally walked straight into an area blocked off with cones . . .

. . . right in time for Felicia and her friends to see me make a fool of myself.

I found Penny and my other friends at the regular table, just as the custodian came over to clean my mess.

"Er, sorry," I said quietly.

My face turned as red as the spaghetti sauce on my shirt. There was a 100 percent chance I was going to end up mentioned in next week's episode of **Real Custodians of Middle School.**

AT LEAST YOU GOT **NOTICED,** BABYMOUSE.

LE SIGH.

Name in Lights

Homeroom. Another thrilling chance to listen to the same old boring announcements. I could pretty much recite them word for word.

GOOD MORNING, STUDENTS. PLEASE LISTEN TO TODAY'S ANNOUNCEMENTS....

"Some friendly reminders: Please stay out of areas blocked off with cones in the cafeteria. Do not bring food or drinks into the library. Cell phones are off-limits while classes are in session."

The announcements droned on:

"The square-dance unit will start next week in gym class. The Audiovisual Club will host its annual tech night next Thursday. Permission slips for the eighth-grade class trip are due on Friday."

Then something caught my ear. . . .

"There will be a meeting after school in the auditorium for the new school play, **Carnival Chaos!**"

A play! That sounded like so much fun. And it could be just the thing I needed to get noticed!

For the rest of the morning, all I could think about was the play. It was impossible to concentrate on my classes. I kept imagining my big break!

☆ ♥ ☆

I could barely contain my excitement at lunch.

"Did you hear the announcements this morning?" I asked my friends.

"You mean the square-dance unit starting in gym?" Wilson asked.

"No," I replied. "The school play! I'm going to try out."

"Oh," said Wilson. "That sounds cool."

"I'm going to try out, too," Georgie added. "After all, I had almost every part in **Au Revoir, My Locker.**"

We all laughed. **Au Revoir, My Locker** was the film I'd written and directed earlier that year. It was . . . an experience.

"The play's going to be very competitive," Penny told us. "A lot of people will want starring roles."

"Bring it on!" I said. "I was born for the stage!"

☆ ♥ ☆

Riiiing!

The moment I had been waiting for all day had arrived. The last bell rang, and it was time for the meeting about **Carnival Chaos!** I ran all the way there, not wanting to miss a second of the action.

But I probably should have just walked.

The meeting was in our giant auditorium. When I first started middle school, I would sometimes go in there to practice monologues or just hang out (that is, until the custodian asked me to stop).

When I got there, I was surprised to see that the auditorium was mostly empty. I had thought everyone in the school would be trying out. **Who doesn't want to be a star, right?**

I walked to the front of the room, where some kids had gathered. The drama teacher, Mr. Russ, was handing out script books. He stopped when he got to me.

"Weren't you the student who directed **Au Revoir, My Locker**?"* he asked.

"Yes!" I exclaimed. "That was me!"

"Oh," he said, clearing his throat. "I see."

*See **Lights, Camera, Middle School!**

I wasn't sure what Mr. Russ meant by that exactly, but I didn't have time to dwell on it, because he clapped his hands for attention.

"Welcome," he began. "I'm so pleased you're interested in getting involved in this year's play, **Carnival Chaos!** It's going to be a lot of fun—and a lot of hard work—"

CREAK!

A loud noise came from the back of the auditorium. Everyone turned to see who was coming in fashionably late through the big wooden doors.

I should have guessed: Felicia Furrypaws and her entourage were making a grand entrance.

"Sorry we're late," Felicia said, sounding very

un-sorry they were late. Her voice carried dramatically across the auditorium.

"It's okay," Mr. Russ said. "I was just going over some housekeeping."

"Housekeeping?" I asked, confused.

"It means **managing**," Mr. Russ explained.

"**Oh,**" I said in the same tone he had used earlier. "**I see.**"

Felicia and her friends took their time walking down the center aisle. When they reached the group, the crowd parted to let them through to the front.

"As I was saying," Mr. Russ continued, "this will be a team effort. And everyone involved in the production will be part of the stage crew."

I didn't know anything about **crew** except that Grampamouse was on a crew team in college. I remembered it involved getting up really early in the morning and rowing a boat full of people a really long way.

"Stage crew assignments will be set design and production, costumes, makeup, props, lighting, and sound," Mr. Russ said. "We will all work together as stagehands to make sure everything runs smoothly."

My mind spun with all the options. This was going to be even better than I thought!

"Finally, tryouts will be right here next Monday after school. You should all choose a scene from the script, and be prepared to perform it in front of an audience," he finished.

My heart leaped. I couldn't wait!

But how could I choose just **one** scene??

☆ ♥ ☆

After dinner that night, I plopped the script onto the kitchen table and sat next to my little brother, Squeak, who was building a card castle.

"Babymouse!" he chirped. "Check this out."

"Squeak, I'm busy right now," I replied without looking up. "I have very important work to do."

I turned to the first page of the script.

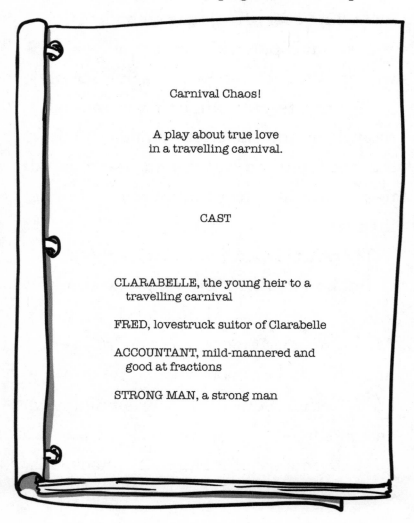

Carnival Chaos!

A play about true love
in a travelling carnival.

CAST

CLARABELLE, the young heir to a
travelling carnival

FRED, lovestruck suitor of Clarabelle

ACCOUNTANT, mild-mannered and
good at fractions

STRONG MAN, a strong man

There was a whole page of characters, but my eyes stopped at Clarabelle. I **had** to be the lead!

But how could I make sure I was chosen? I definitely needed all the help I could get.

"Who could give me some acting tips?" I wondered aloud.

"What about Georgie?" Squeak asked. "He's a really good actor."

I had forgotten my little brother was still there. He had built a giant card castle almost the size of his entire body!

"That's it!" I said, pounding my hands on the table.

The card castle collapsed, and cards fluttered everywhere.

"Oops," I said. "Sorry, Squeak."

Squeak scowled. "You can make it up to me."

I picked up my phone and texted Georgie.

Halp! How do I land a lead?

Mesmerize your lines

?!?!

I mean, MEMORIZE
your lines.
Stupid autocorrect.

lol

I needed someone to rehearse my lines with.

"Mom!" I yelled.

"In here, Babymouse," she called back.

She was in her office next to a big stack of paperwork.

"I'm trying out for the play," I said. "Can you help me rehearse my lines?"

"I would love to, honey, but I have to finish paying all these bills," she replied. "Why don't you see what your dad is doing?"

Le sigh.

I found Dad in the laundry room, matching up socks.

"Hey, Babymouse," he said. "Did you come to help me fold laundry?"

"Um, no," I replied. "I need to practice my lines for the school play."

"Ah," he replied. "I still have a lot more laundry to do. Did you try asking Mom?"

Le double sigh.

Out of options, I went back into the kitchen and found Squeak. As if he knew I was in a bind, he smiled the biggest smile he could smile.

I decided to text Wilson.

Halp! I need someone 2 rehearse my lines with

I would but I have too much hw

:(

Y don't u rent the movie?

!!!

Watching the movie seemed like the perfect shortcut. I could watch the same scene over and over until I had it down pat.

I went into the living room and turned on the smart TV.

"Babymouse," Dad called from the laundry room, "no TV until your homework is done."

"It's done. Can I rent a movie?" I asked, then quickly added the magic words: "It's for school."

"Okay," Dad replied. "Let Squeak watch with you."

"Do I have to?" I groaned.

"Yes," he replied. "It will be fun. You can pretend you're at the movies."

In seconds, Squeak was by my side with a bowl of popcorn.

I followed the instructions to rent the movie over the internet. Soon, it was set up and we were ready to watch.

"Hold on," Squeak said, and went into our parents' room.

He returned wearing a top hat and sat down directly in front of me.

"Squeak, I can't see!" I complained.

"I know," he replied. "Just like at the real movies!"

We both laughed, and he took off his hat.

Finally, Squeak and I started watching.

The movie was really funny, but not what I was expecting at all.

When the final scene began, Mom walked into the room.

"Bedtime," she announced.

Parents have a way of making you go to bed at the worst possible times.

"Mom, there's just fifteen minutes left," I told her.

"Perfect!" she replied. "You can watch it after school tomorrow."

The next day, everyone was buzzing about **Carnival Chaos!** spoilers. I had to cover my ears all day so the ending wouldn't be ruined for me.

When I got home, I immediately turned on the TV and set up the movie. Right as I was about to press PLAY, Mom walked in.

"Aren't you going to wait for Squeak to finish watching?" she asked.

"But, Mom," I pleaded, "I'm dying to know the ending. I spent all day avoiding spoilers!"

"He'll be home right after his piano lesson," she replied. "It would be nice for you to wait."

"Ugh!" I replied. "Fine."

Being a good big sister was really the worst sometimes.

Squeak got home one **whole** hour later.

"Want to watch the end of the movie?" I asked as soon as he walked in the door.

"No, thanks," Squeak replied. "I already know all the Martians die."

AHHHH!!!!

AT LEAST I DIDN'T SPOIL IT FOR YOU, BABYMOUSE.

☆ ♡ ☆

I watched the movie literally every single night for the rest of the week (and yes, I cried every time the Martians died). Finally, I felt like I had my lines down **perfectly.**

The night before the audition, I handed Mom the script and asked her to follow along with the first scene.

"In this scene," I explained, "I will be abducted by aliens right before the sun sets."

Mom frowned. She flipped through the pages of the book.

"Babymouse, I don't see that part here."

"It should be the first page," I said.

Mom shook her head and showed me the first scene.

"In fact," she said, still flipping through the script, "I've seen this play before, and I don't remember anything about aliens."

"But . . . it was in the movie!"

Mom and I pulled up the movie on our TV.

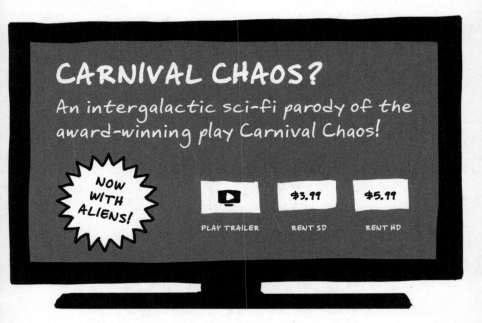

CARNIVAL CHAOS?
An intergalactic sci-fi parody of the award-winning play Carnival Chaos!

NOW WITH ALIENS!

$3.99
$5.99

PLAY TRAILER   RENT SD   RENT HD

"A **parody**?!" I exclaimed. "I can't believe I've been watching a **parody** this whole time!"

I turned to Mom. "What is a parody anyway?" I asked.

"It's basically a spoof or joke that makes fun of the original," she explained.

I smacked myself in the forehead. I had been so excited to get started rehearsing, I didn't make sure the lines in the movie were the same as in the script for the play.

My stomach dropped. So much for my shortcut.

Now I was really in a pickle!

COULDN'T HELP MYSELF.

I DON'T HAVE TIME FOR THIS!

I had no choice but to do all my rehearsing in one night.

Squeak agreed to rehearse with me, but only after I promised him a batch of cupcakes.

I, Babymouse, promise my AMAZING brother Squeak two dozen cupcakes in the following flavors:

- Vanilla
- Chocolate
- Strawberry
- Raspberry
- Lemon
- Peanut butter
- Nacho cheese
- Mashed potato

BLECH!

Babymouse ♡

But even my old-fashioned rehearsing didn't go as planned. We just had one copy of the script, and passing it back and forth was frustrating.

"This is taking too long," Squeak complained. "What's my motivation?"

"Cupcakes," I reminded him.

"How do I know you're **really** going to make them for me?"

"Okay," I told him. "I have an idea. I will make the cupcakes"—I ripped the pages out of the script book and handed them to Squeak—"but in the meantime, can you cut up the dialogue and glue my lines on one piece of paper and yours on another?"

"No problem," Squeak said.

The first batch of cupcakes was done just as Squeak finished the pasting.

Finally, everything was ready to go.

We practiced the scene and stuffed our faces until Mom came in and put an end to the cupcake-a-thon.

"And . . . SCENE!" she said, smiling. "Time for bed, you two."

I went upstairs, feeling relieved for the first time all week. I knew the lines backward and forward. (Literally! Squeak accidentally glued some upside down.)

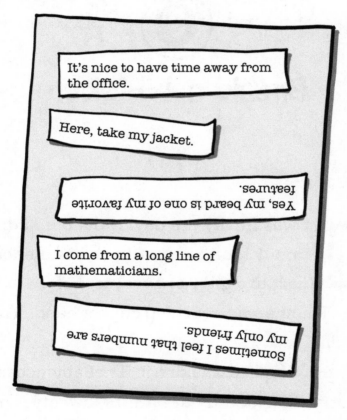

It's nice to have time away from the office.

Here, take my jacket.

Yes, my beard is one of my favorite features.

I come from a long line of mathematicians.

Sometimes I feel that numbers are my only friends.

As I drifted off to sleep that night, I dreamed of Broadway. . . .

Break a Whisker

It was finally the day of the big audition. I found a seat in the audience
next to a girl I'd never met before.

"Hi," she said, reaching out her hand. "I'm
Millie."

"Hi," I replied, shaking it. "I'm Babymouse.
Sorry if my hands are a little sweaty. I'm
pretty nervous."

She laughed.

"Don't worry," she said. "I think we're all nervous."

She pointed to the rest of our row, where everyone was looking pretty rough.

"What part are you trying out for?" she asked.

"I want to be Clarabelle," I told her. "I've been practicing her lines all week."

"That's great!" she replied. "I think you'd make a great Clarabelle."

"Thanks," I replied. "What do you want to be?"

"Believe it or not, I want to be the strong man."

"Really?" I asked, laughing.

"Yep," she responded. "I've been working out." She flexed her biceps, and we both laughed. In no time, we were cracking up and pretending to be bodybuilders. We were so busy goofing around ("Inside voices, please!") that I didn't notice how many kids had already tried out.

Someone tapped me on the shoulder.

I turned around and saw Georgie.

"Babymouse, you're on deck," he said.

He pointed toward the front row, where I saw a whole line of my classmates dressed like Clarabelle.

I couldn't believe it. It was like everyone wanted the same part!

"Break a leg, Babymouse," Millie said.

Gulp!

I bounced from foot to foot as I waited near the stage.

Suddenly, a voice boomed over the loud-speaker, "You're next, Babymouse."

I looked over to see Mr. Russ at the judges' table, holding a microphone and a clipboard.

This was my one chance. I could not give up now.

I held my head high and went onstage. Raj, a friendly fox I recognized from the cafeteria, handed me the microphone.

"Did you forget your script?" Mr. Russ asked over the loudspeaker. "You can borrow one."

"I actually don't need it," I replied loudly into the microphone. "I mesmerized my lines."

Felicia and her crew laughed loudly from the front row.

I took a deep breath.

"I mean I **memorized** my lines."

Mr. Russ smiled. "That's very impressive, Babymouse," he said. "Begin whenever you're ready."

The next two minutes were a total blur.

I laughed!

I cried!

I emoted emotion!

I even tap-danced!

As I said my lines, I became Clarabelle. This was the part I was born to play, that only I could be!

I was . . . Baby-Clarabelle!

When I was finished, I walked back to my seat triumphantly.

"How'd I do?" I asked Millie.

"Umm . . . I thought you were reading for Clarabelle?" Millie replied.

"I did," I said, confused.

Millie shook her head. "You said the wrong lines," she told me.

"What do you mean?" I asked.

"You read the accountant's lines, Babymouse."

I thought back to the night before.

How could I not have realized Squeak and I had mixed up the roles?

I couldn't believe it. I had learned all the wrong lines—again!

Typical.

☆ ♡ ☆

It was too late to do anything about my mistake, so I would just have to cross my fingers and hope for the best.

Luckily, I didn't have to wait too long.

Mr. Russ posted the results of the audition before school the next day.

CARNIVAL CHAOS!

AUDITION RESULTS

CLARABELLE .... FELICIA

FRED .... GEORGIE

ACCOUNTANT ... BERRY

STRONG MAN .... MILLIE

"I can't believe I got the part of Fred!" Georgie exclaimed.

"And I got the part of the strong man!" Millie yelled.

They were both so excited that they high-fived, even though they didn't know each other.

I couldn't believe it. It was bad enough that I didn't get the part of Clarabelle. But to not even get the part I **accidentally** tried out for? Typical.

As if she could read my mind, I heard Berry complaining.

"Ugh!" she groaned. "Accountant is the worst part of all!"

"Not really," said Felicia. "You could always be Clown #2."

Felicia and her friends laughed as they turned to look at me.

I searched the list again. At the very bottom, after three "junior accountants," four "nonflying elephants," and one "unnamed boat rower," I found my name.

JR. ACCT. #3 .... LOGAN

CLOWN #1 .... LOCKER

CLOWN #2 .... BABYMOUSE

I looked over to see Locker slamming into things excitedly.

I was pretty grumpy all morning. I made it through my classes until lunch, when I could see my friends. At least that would take my mind off my bad luck. Or so I thought . . .

"Did they post the audition results?" Penny asked.

"Yeah," Georgie replied. "I got the part of Fred!"

"That's one of the leads!" Penny exclaimed. "Congratulations!"

Georgie beamed proudly.

"Babymouse got a role, too," he said after a minute.

Everyone turned to look at me.

"I'm, um, Clown #2," I told them.

"That's great, Babymouse," Wilson said. "How many clowns are there?"

"Two."

"Oh, um, well—that's great!"

"I know you wanted to be Clarabelle,"

Penny told me. "But I think you'll make a great Clown #2!"

"Thanks, Penny," I replied. "It wasn't what I wanted, but you're right. I can be the best Clown #2 this school has ever seen."

"That's the spirit!" Penny said. "How many lines do you have?"

I flipped through the script.

"One line?" I cried. "I only have ONE LINE?!?!"

"What's the line, Babymouse?" Penny asked.

If only a clown were here!

CLOWN # 2
Peas are tasty, but I prefer artichokes.

I DON'T EVEN LIKE ARTICHOKES!!!!!

YOU WILL DEFINITELY GET A TONY AWARD FOR THIS ROLE, BABYMOUSE.

Crew-zing

It was the first day of rehearsal.

I moved my scrambled eggs across the plate and back again. I hadn't eaten a bite.

"Babymouse, you need fuel for your big day," Dad said.

"I'm not hungry," I said with a sigh.

"Now, remember, Babymouse," Mom said. "There are no small roles. Only small actors."

That was easy for her to say! Mom had always gotten the lead in her high school productions. She was also a cheerleader and the president of the student council. I'd seen pictures of her in the old yearbooks in the attic.

"But, Mom," I said, throwing up my hands. "My role isn't even small—it's **petite**!"

"In that case," Squeak said, "there are no petite roles, only petite actors!"

Mom and Dad laughed, but I just rolled my eyes.

As the day wore on, I became more and more excited about rehearsal. Even if I wasn't the **star** of the show, I could still be a sparkly asteroid. Or a shooting star. Or something.

By the time the last bell rang, I bounced into the theater, full of energy.

Mr. Russ led everyone onto the stage, where a big folding table had been set up.

"To start off," he explained, "we're going to do what's called a 'table read.'"

... WHEREFORE ART THOU ROMEO?

As if he had seen what was in my head, Mr. Russ continued, "This means we'll go through the script as a group, with everyone reading their parts aloud."

I was pretty excited.

I took a seat between Georgie and Millie, and students filled in around us.

The read began, and at first, it was pretty cool. But after a while, I realized it was mostly Felicia talking, and that got kind of annoying. Especially because she had many lines that I felt I could say a lot more dramatically.

Unfortunately, my one line wasn't until the very end, and all I could think about was how to say it **perfectly.**

60

The kids droned on and on. At the super-slow rate we were going, we wouldn't make it to my line before they locked up the school for the night!

Halfway through the read, Mr. Russ told us to take a short break to "perk up."

Everyone stampeded to the vending machine for a snack.

I dug through my backpack for cash, but all I had was, well, nothing.

Millie walked over to me.

"Need some help?" she asked.

"I was looking for spare change, but I think I spent my last dollar on a side of Tater Tots with lunch."

"I had those, too," Millie said with a laugh. "Here, I'll buy you something from the vending machine."

"That's really nice of you," I replied. "Thanks!"

We got on line.

SHEESH. HOW MANY PEOPLE ARE EVEN IN THIS PLAY?

PUSH

By the time it was our turn, the only things left were a pack of almonds, breath mints, and strawberry gum.

Typical.

I dropped in my money and pushed the button for the strawberry gum.

"Break's over!" Mr. Russ hollered.

We all trooped back into the room.

As the table reading continued, I started chewing a piece of gum. It was pretty good, so I popped another in my mouth. That one was good, too, so I had one more. Before I knew it, I was chewing the whole pack!

But even that couldn't help with the boredom of listening to kids drone on and on in a monotone. I mindlessly started to twirl the gum on my finger. There was so much of it, though, that my gum art got pretty elaborate.

That's when it happened: I lost control of the gum, and it got all over my face and whiskers!

And **of course**, right at that moment, it was finally my turn to read.

"Clown #2?" Mr. Russ prompted.

I tried to open my mouth, but it was hopeless.

"Mwah-mwah-mwah, mwah-mwah-mwah" was all that came out.

OH, BABYMOUSE.

TYPIC-MWAH.

☆ ♡ ☆

I excused myself to go to the bathroom. Or I **would** have if I could have gotten actual words out.

I tried to get the gum off using soap and water, but that didn't help much. Then I tried using hand sanitizer, but that just stung and made my face even more irritated. I gave up and dried my face with paper towels, and bits of paper got stuck all over the gum.

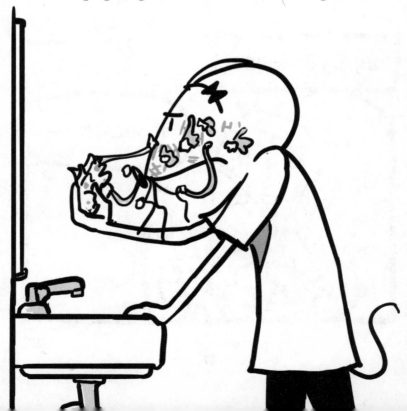

Just when I thought things couldn't get worse, Felicia walked into the bathroom.

"Need help?" she asked.

"Well, actually, yeah," I replied.

"That's too bad," she said, walking into a stall with a cackle.

I checked my phone to see what I could do to remove the gum, and it turned out peanut butter was supposed to help. But where could I get peanut butter? I remembered that gross peanut butter sandwich in my backpack, so I did the best I could to get the gum off with it.

It was not my finest moment. But it worked!

At least they were finishing the read by the time I got back.

"Excellent job, everyone," Mr. Russ said, giving a small round of applause. "Keep reading through your lines to familiarize yourself with the script."

He stood up and took a clipboard from his bag.

"The last thing we'll do is sign up for crew positions," he continued. "We will need teams for wardrobe, makeup, props, set design and production, lighting, and sound.

The sign-up sheet is on this clipboard. Please pass it around and add your name to the position you would like."

No one moved. A lone snoring sound came from the other end of the table.

"Did I mention sign-ups are first come, first served?"

Immediately, everyone sprang to life and pounced on the clipboard.

It was like a football pileup, with Mr. Russ's clipboard as the ball.

Felicia plucked the clipboard from a hand at the bottom of the pile. "It's only natural that I be in charge of makeup," she said, adding her name in huge letters.

"And I'll do costumes," Melinda added.

"Makeup **and** costumes for me!" Berry exclaimed.

Hmm, I thought. **Those sound fun!**

But by the time I could get to the clipboard, all the makeup and costume positions had been taken. In fact, there were only two openings left. **Le sigh.**

Costumes ___Melinda___ ___Berry___

Sets _____

Lighting _____

I SEEM TO RECALL YOU ONCE HAD A LIGHTING ISSUE, BABYMOUSE.

ZWOOM!

"Maybe you should do sets, Babymouse," Georgie suggested.

"Right," I agreed, signing my name. "I think that's a good idea."

Just then, Felicia and her friends walked by. "You would never catch **me** signing up for set crew," Felicia said, loudly enough for everyone to hear.

"Power tools are scary!" Melinda added.

"And you get dirty," Berry replied. "Gross!"

"Actually, power tools are awesome!" Georgie corrected.

"Yeah," Millie agreed. "I like fixing stuff **and** doing makeup."

Hmm, I thought. **Maybe sets will be kind of cool after all.**

Exercise Schmexercise

The next day at rehearsal, Mr. Russ gathered everyone in the middle of the stage.

"Today we're going to do an exercise," he told us.

"Exercise?!?!?" I grumbled to Millie. "I **hate** exercise."

There was nothing fun about jumping around (or falling, in my case). Not to mention, being sweaty was the worst.

NNGH!

NOW, THAT'S WHAT I CALL LEARNING THE ROPES.

"They're actually **acting** exercises," Millie whispered.

Phew!

I breathed a sigh of relief.

"First, we are going to do some face warm-ups," Mr. Russ said.

I began rubbing my face as much as possible. Soon, my cheeks were bright pink.

"That should be warm enough," I whispered.

Millie giggled and shook her head. She pointed to Mr. Russ, who was passing out small mirrors.

Oh.

I smiled sheepishly and took a mirror from the box. Looking in the mirror, I tried not to focus on my messy whiskers.

"She'll probably break it just by looking at it," Felicia whispered to her friends. Berry and Melinda giggled.

Then my face turned really pink. I tried to ignore Felicia and focus on what Mr. Russ was saying.

"Hold up your mirror and make dramatic expressions," Mr. Russ said. "Let's start with **sad.** You need to be authentic, so try to remember an occasion when you felt sadness."

Thanks to Felicia's snarky line, I had no problem making a sad face. I thought of all the mean things Felicia and her friends had said or done to me over the years. My face transformed, and tears began to well up in my eyes. (I was really getting into this acting thing!)

"Great work, Babymouse!" Mr. Russ said. "Very sincere."

But I didn't stop there. I kept thinking about all the other things that had made me sad.

I decided to try **angry** next. But I guess
I was being a little overdramatic. . . .

"Now continue the exercise using other dramatic emotions," Mr. Russ said. "I'm going to walk around and give you feedback."

"Now we'll move to a classic tongue-twister exercise," Mr. Russ continued.

Betty bought a bit of butter,
but the bit of butter Betty bought was bitter,
so Betty bought a bit of better butter
to make the bit of bitter butter better.

He made it sound easy, but when it was our turn, most kids couldn't even get past the first line.

The more I thought about it, the more confused I became.

If the butter was bitter in the first place, why would Betty buy more?

Wasn't the second batch of butter likely to be bitter, too?

Why didn't Betty just return the first batch and buy margarine or olive oil?

Or, butter yet (oops—better yet!), go to a different store?

There were so many questions bouncing around in my head that I couldn't concentrate on the tongue twister anymore.

Mr. Russ came over, and I asked if I could make up my own tongue twister. One that made more **sense** to me.

"Sure, Babymouse," he said. "Let's hear it."

Babymouse bought a bunch of berries,
like blueberries, blackberries,
and boysenberries.
Babymouse baked the berries
into a berry batter
using bits of Betty's better butter.

"That's a berry—I mean **very**—creative way of expressing yourself, Babymouse," said Mr. Russ. "In fact, it gives me an idea for an extra assignment tonight."

Everyone groaned.

"Tonight, each of you should write your

own silly tongue twister, and practice it over
and over until you can recite it perfectly."

Everyone glared at me.

MAYBE THEY'RE JUST
PRACTICING THEIR
ANGRY FACES?

☆ ♥ ☆

That night, I was at the dinner table with my family. I was so busy thinking about the play that I had barely touched my food.

"How was school today?" Dad asked.

"Good," I replied, still lost in a daydream.

"How was your homework?" he continued.

"Good," I replied again.

"How are your vegetables?" Mom asked, smirking.

"Good," I repeated.

"We're thinking of moving to Mars next month," Mom added.

"Good," I replied—then came to my senses. "Wait, **what**?!"

I looked up to see Mom, Dad, and Squeak all smiling at me.

"Er, I guess I am kind of wrapped up in the play tonight."

"That's okay," Mom laughed. "I'm just glad my veggies are such a hit!"

"How are the play rehearsals going?" Dad asked.

My brain flooded with a million thoughts again.

"Can you pass the butter, please?" Squeak asked.

Stage Where?

The next day, I decided to wear a beret to school.

"What's with the hat?" Wilson asked. He took it off my head and tried it on.

"It's a beret," I explained. "I'm in the **thee-a-tah** now."

"Got it," Wilson replied. "Want to hang out after school?"

"Can't. I have a **thee-a-tah** rehearsal," I replied.

"Okay," Wilson said. "Next time."

At rehearsal, my head spun as Mr. Russ explained stage directions. I'd learned about them in my elementary school musical, but they were still so confusing! I kept bumping into people and stepping on toes, including Felicia's.

"Babymouse!" Felicia barked at me. "You are so frustrating. Just do the total opposite of whatever it is you're doing!"

"That's not very nice, Felicia," Mr. Russ said. "But what Felicia is trying to explain, Babymouse, is that 'stage right' is on the audience's left. Get it?"

"Uh . . . maybe?" I said.

Now I felt embarrassed **and** totally lost.

Millie must have noticed my exasperation, because she took my hand and led me through the directions.

"Now that we've gotten the directions down," Mr. Russ continued, "it's time to work on listening for your **cue**. A cue is something that prompts you to come out onstage."

Millie pointed to the line in the script right before my line.

"Here's your cue," she whispered.

If only a clown were here!

CLOWN # 2
Peas are tasty, but I prefer artichokes.

I guess as far as cue lines go, mine was pretty easy to remember. Still, I read the line over and over until my vision started to go blurry. I didn't want to make any more mistakes if I could help it.

"Now wait in the wings while I call out your cues," Mr. Russ said.

We practiced for a while until everyone knew their cues by heart. Then Mr. Russ started yelling them out randomly, to test whether people could remember them.

"If only a clown were here!" Mr. Russ yelled.

That was my cue!

BABYMOUSE

In Her World-Premiere Performance as

CLOWN #2

I rushed onstage in a flurry. Locker was already there—and, man, did he look impatient. **(SLAM! SLAM!)**

"I'm here! I'm here!" I yelled triumphantly.

"I'm glad you know your cue, Babymouse, but that's not your line," Mr. Russ corrected me. "Please learn your line!"

Yikes.

"Oh, right, sorry."

THAT'S THEE-A-TAH FOR YOU, BABYMOUSE.

MEEP.

Hammer Time

Crew day had arrived. I was still a little bummed that I hadn't gotten on the makeup or costume crew. But I had an idea. I asked Penny to give me a dramatic makeover after school, just in time for play practice.

STAGE ENTRANCE

CREW DAY

BEFORE

AFTER

I wore my prettiest dress and highest heels to the auditorium.

"Babymouse, what on earth are you wearing?" Georgie asked when he saw me in the hallway.

"I'm practicing theater hair, makeup, and costumes," I replied.

"But I thought you were on set construction," he said, confused.

"Oh, I am," I admitted. "But I'm hoping Mr. Russ will be so impressed that he'll let me switch to hair or makeup or costumes."

Just then, Mr. Russ clapped his hands and gathered us in the center of the room.

"Okay, we're going to break up into teams and get to work on our projects. Remember, safety first!"

"Set crew!" yelled Raj. Millie and I headed over.

"Mr. Russ put me in charge of the set-construction team," he said. "Today we'll be building platforms for the actors."

"Is that why you wore those **platform** shoes, Babymouse?" Felicia snickered as she walked by with a list of characters.

I frowned, looking at my high heels.

Raj scrutinized my shoes as well.

"Hmm," he said, "those don't seem like the **best** footwear for constructing sets. Why don't you go into the back utility closet, and you can borrow my old steel-toe work boots."

Ugh. This was definitely not going as planned.

"Oh, uh, okay," I agreed, trying to hide my disappointment.

I **clunk-clunk-clunk**ed backstage in my heels. That was the first time I noticed how many closets were behind the stage!

It was like a TV game show, where every door hid fabulous prizes! If, you know, the fabulous prizes were things like brooms, mops, and boxes of cleaning supplies.

Then I saw Felicia and her friends in the wardrobe closet. It was the biggest closet I had ever seen!

There were rows and rows of every fabric and every color under the rainbow. It was like the show **Backstages of the Rich and Famous.**

(You know, if that **was** a show.)

I had to be a part of it!

I walked toward the door, just in time for Felicia to slam it in my face.

I had no choice but to find Raj's steel-toe work boots and head back to my group.

"Do you know how to use a hammer?" Raj asked.

"Ummmm," I replied.

I didn't exactly want to answer that question.

NOT LONG AGO.

THWACK!
THWACK!
THWACK!

STRAIGHTEN OUT, WHISKERS!

"Well, I can teach you," he said.

He handed me safety goggles and demonstrated the proper form for hammering. When he was done, he gave me some plywood and nails and told me I could get started.

Let me tell you: I had no idea how much effort it takes to put a play together. Check out my montage!

I MEASURED.

I SAWED.

I SCREWED.

I DRILLED.

I SANDED.

I PAINTED.

I EVEN **WHATEVER-THIS-THING-IS-E**

I was really starting to get the hang of building now. It was—dare I say it?—fun!

Just when I thought I was happy to have gotten this gig, Raj made an unusual suggestion.

"Do you want to go backstage and grab a belt?" he asked.

"That's a great idea!" I replied. "There's no reason we can't be a little festive while we work."

He gave me a funny look, but I was already on my way backstage to check out the wardrobe room.

I knocked, but there was no answer. I tried the knob. To my surprise, it opened!

I realized Felicia and her friends were probably off doing makeup. That meant I had the whole place to myself. I picked up a glittery, sparkly belt to give me a bit of disco flair.

When I got back, Raj gave me another funny look.

"What's that for?" he asked.

"You said to grab a belt," I reminded him.

He grinned and went backstage. In a couple of minutes, he was back with a new accessory for me.

Let's just say I was **way** off.

BLECH.

Like I said, building sets was fun and cool. But I couldn't help but wonder what the other crew positions were like.

The sound folks kept coming over the loudspeaker, "testing" the equipment by telling jokes and quoting funny movie lines.

The lighting folks were playing with all the colorful stage lights. (Though Mr. Russ had to tell them to cool it with the spotlights. Literally! It was getting really hot onstage.)

And, of course, I couldn't keep my eyes from longingly gazing backstage to watch what Felicia and her friends were doing in the wardrobe department. They seemed to be having so much fun as they tried on lots of cool armor and over-the-top outfits.

Needless to say, I wasn't **exactly** paying the most attention. When I looked down, I realized I'd hammered my skirt to a piece of plywood.

TYPICAL.

IT'S **KIND OF** BEDAZZLED.

☆ ♡ ☆

A bit later, Raj told us we could take a break from the platforms and move on to painting backdrops.

It was a nice day outside, so we decided to carry the canvases to the back parking lot.

"Just be careful to always use the door-stop, because otherwise the door will slam shut and lock automatically," Raj cautioned us.

We carried the canvases past the dump-ster and got to work.

"Babymouse, can you paint this?" Raj asked. He held up a beautiful picture of a sunset on a lake.

"No problem!" I replied.

I took the picture from him and started setting up my paints.

"Why do I only have one shade of pink?" I asked, dismayed. "I can't work like this!"

"Don't you want to use pencil to sketch it out first?" Raj asked.

"Please, Raj," I replied. "You don't want to stifle an artist's creativity, do you?"

He made a face like he wasn't sure how to respond.

"Okay," he said finally. "Just . . . you know. Nothing too **experimental,** okay?"

"You got it," I said, nodding.

I don't know what he was so worried about. It just so happens that I was recently chosen as a featured student artist.*

It was true, though, that I didn't have a lot of experience painting landscapes. My previous work had mostly followed a certain . . . theme.

*See **School-Tripped.**

Babymouse ♡

Babymouse ♡

Babymouse ♡

Babymouse ♡

Babymouse ♡

Babymouse ♡

Inspired by some of the greatest painters of all time, I got right to work.

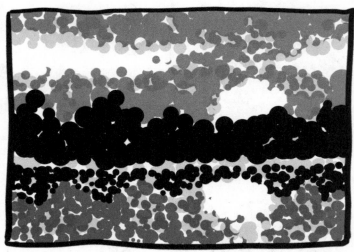

BORING-ISM . . .

Painting was fun, and even though Raj wanted the least creative option, it did look pretty good by the end.

Apparently, he agreed.

"You have a great eye, Babymouse," he said.

"Thanks," I replied, surprised.

Finally, it was time to go home. As we cleaned up the paints, I thought about how much we'd gotten done in only one day.

I was glad to be able to help out and feel like part of the team.

Plus, I liked the idea of having my art in giant canvases onstage. It was almost like my painting had a starring role, all on its own.

Once the mess was (mostly) clean, the whole construction crew washed up and got ready to walk out together.

"Great work today, team!" Raj said, giving us all high fives.

On my way out the door, I passed a mirror and saw how sweaty, dirty, and covered in paint (painty?) I was. Of course, right at that moment, Felicia and her friends swaggered by with perfectly coiffed whiskers and freshly applied makeup.

Wardrobe Unfitting?

As the days (and weeks!) passed, the production went into full swing. It was finally time for the cast to get costumes and makeup.

"Now, remember," Mr. Russ said, "always put on your costume BEFORE you do your makeup. This is very important."

I was so excited! I'd finally get to have my very own wardrobe fitting. I couldn't wait to see what kind of costume I would get to wear. I knew Clown #2 was probably not going to get a cool space suit or fancy gown, but maybe it would be **something** interesting.

But when I saw the clown costume, my worst fears were realized. . . .

Great, I thought. **Now I'm going to have nightmares about myself.**

Problems with my clown costume:

(1) Super baggy (also probably a fire hazard!)

(2) More holes than a slice of Swiss cheese

(3) Smelled like it had been worn by a hundred other kids . . .

(4) . . . who had never worn deodorant.

I begged Mr. Russ to let me change costumes, but he was no help at all.

"You're playing the part of a clown, Babymouse," he said. "What did you expect?"

"I was hoping for a fabulous French clown costume!" I told him.

"Sorry," he replied. "There was only one of those, and it went to Clown #1."

☆ ♥ ☆

I didn't have much chance to complain because I was rushed off to the makeup room. Time for stage makeup!

Felicia was across the room, working on another student. But she dropped what she was doing and made a beeline for me as soon as I walked in.

At first, I thought she was going to tease me about my terrible clown costume, but I was wrong.

"Can I do your makeup, Babymouse?" she asked sweetly.

"Um . . ." I bit my lip, unsure. "Do you really want to?" I asked.

"Of course!" she replied. "Your look will be truly one of a kind!"

"Uh, okay," I agreed.

She took my hand and whisked me off to an old-fashioned makeup chair. Students zigzagged around us, looking for blush sticks and fake eyelashes.

In the middle of the chaos, Mr. Russ was trying to explain the basics of stage makeup.

"It exaggerates your face so the audience can see you more clearly," Mr. Russ explained. "You've all heard the phrase 'Less is more.' Well, with stage makeup, **more** is more!"

I liked the sound of that! Finally, I would get a real makeover, with dramatic results.

Felicia wasted no time in getting to work.

I squirmed to look at the mirror, but it was too hard to see over her shoulder.

"Sit still, Babymouse," Felicia huffed. "You can see when I'm done."

"Start by applying foundation all over the face!" Mr. Russ yelled. He continued shouting advice to anyone still listening.

Fill in eyebrows with powder!

Use dark liner on the lips!

Apply ample blush to the apples of the cheeks!

Add fake eyelashes for dramatic flair!

I sat patiently for as long as I could. It was so frustrating not being able to see Felicia's progress. But I reminded myself of what I'd told Raj about not stifling an artist's creativity.

After what felt like **forever**, Felicia finally put down her brushes.

"Okay," she said. "Are you ready for the big reveal?"

Before I could answer, she stepped out of the way so I could see myself in the vanity mirror.

I screamed, and Mr. Russ rushed over.

Surely, he would be able to see how awful I looked. But I was wrong.

"That's excellent, Felicia!" he exclaimed. "Great use of color and shading."

I felt like I was going to die. But that's when it got **worse.**

Mr. Russ clapped his hands.

"Attention!" he said. "Please look at Felicia's perfect use of clown makeup on Babymouse. Truly horrifying result."

Everyone turned to look at me. Their faces confirmed that I looked absolutely terrifying.

I excused myself to go to the bathroom. I should have expected what happened next. . . .

☆ ♥ ☆

Finally, rehearsal was over.

"That's it for today, everyone," Mr. Russ said. "Make sure you take off the stage makeup as soon as you get home."

He didn't have to tell me twice. I couldn't wait to get that makeup off!

But when I got home, I remembered I had a **ton** of homework. I quickly scarfed down dinner, and then locked myself in my bedroom for the whole evening to get it done.

I got tired of sitting at my desk, and took my work to my bed and settled down. I just had to annotate two chapters of this book, and then I would be done. . . .

The next thing I knew, my alarm was going off. Huh?

I had fallen asleep in my bed while studying.

"You better get moving, Babymouse!" my mom called.

My face was all red and splotchy under the makeup. I had developed a reaction from having the makeup on for so long!

I frowned in the mirror as I looked at my swollen red face. It was almost as bad as the clown makeup. **Almost.**

I was hoping it didn't look as bad as I thought it did. Maybe I was overreacting. But when I got downstairs to breakfast, I was convinced otherwise.

Squeak told me I should use makeup to cover my face. I would have rolled my eyes if I'd been able to move them.

Glow in the Dark

I begged Mom to let me stay home, but she told me there was no reason to miss school just because I was embarrassed.

"Besides," she said, "you're not sick with anything contagious."

If only she could have seen the looks of horror on everyone's faces the day before!

Instead, Mom gave me a face-calming cream, which she said would make the swelling go down eventually. But that didn't help in the meantime. . . .

By rehearsal, things were back to normal—just in time for me to have the makeup redone.

Mr. Russ clapped his hands loudly, and everyone gathered around.

"Today I want to go over how to change sets between scenes," he said. "Everyone who is not on deck for the next scene will have to pitch in."

Ugh, I thought. **With my one line, I am barely in any scenes!**

I guessed that meant I'd better get used to some heavy lifting.

"The house lights will go to completely black," he continued. "So the glow tape on the stage floor will show you where to find the furniture and other props."

Glow tape? I wondered.

As if in response, he held up a roll of reflective tape.

"Can I get a volunteer to put the glow tape on the stage?"

No one raised their hand.

"It should be an easy task," he said. "You just make sure to hit all the marks on this sheet." He held up a paper with lots of "X" marks on it.

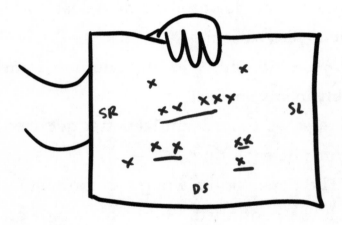

"All those X's remind me of a treasure hunt," I whispered to Millie.

Millie giggled, and Mr. Russ turned toward me. (I guess I needed to work on my whisper volume. . . .)

"Babymouse, was that you volunteering? Excellent!" he said before I could respond. He handed me the sheet and the roll of tape.

Le sigh.

We were getting close to opening night, so everyone broke off to do assorted odds and ends.

I started taping the floor, according to the directions. Mr. Russ was right—it was pretty easy after all!

But my daydream caused me to trip over a microphone wire, and I dropped the paper. When I picked it up, the stage diagram was upside down, and I noticed that the layout was reversed. And when I looked closely, I saw a tiny "SL" and "SR," for "stage left" and "stage right."

Oh no! I had done the whole job backward.

I began pulling up the tape, hoping no one would notice.

No luck there.

I started taping everything all over again. Then a delicious smell began wafting through the air, distracting me from my work. Soon, Raj poked his head through the curtain.

"Looks good!" he said, pointing toward the tape.

"Smells good!" I replied with a grin.

"Yeah, I came to tell you the set crew ordered pizza and soda, and it just got here. Want some?"

"Totally!" I replied.

I followed him to a classroom where the set crew was chowing down. They had already eaten three pizzas!

Seeing the empty pizza boxes made me think of Pizza Kitty, the tiny kitten Penny and I rescued on our class trip into the city.*

*See **School-Tripped**.

I told everyone the story of Pizza Kitty, and all about our Big City adventure. Soon, they were laughing and asking me lots of questions about her.

I meant to go back to glow-taping, but everyone else started telling funny stories, and I got sidetracked.

Mr. Russ came in to check on us.

"Ready to practice moving the sets?" he asked.

Everyone groaned, mouths and tummies full, and took the last sip of their sodas.

I had this nagging feeling that I had forgotten something, but I couldn't remember what it was.

Oh well, I thought. If it was important, I would remember eventually.

☆ ♡ ☆

The next day, Mr. Russ moved me to costumes instead of sets.

I wondered if it was because of the glow
tape fiasco, but tried to tell myself he had
finally recognized my fabulous style.

In any case, this was fine with me because I got to spend more time with Millie!

Mr. Russ gathered the costume crew in the giant wardrobe closet.

I tried to focus on what he was saying instead of staring at all the sparkly sequined gowns, shiny metal armor, and fluffy tulle tutus.

"Now, as the lead," Mr. Russ said, "Felicia will have several costume changes. And they will be 'quick changes.' Does anyone know what that means?"

I raised my hand.

"Like when you take your car to the shop, and they promise to change the oil in less than twenty minutes or it's free?"

Everyone laughed except Mr. Russ.

"Good one, Babymouse," Millie said with a smile. She raised her hand, and Mr. Russ called on her.

"A quick change is when an actor has to change costumes quickly between scenes, so the costumes are specially designed for that. We did it during a talent show at summer camp."

"Precisely!" Mr. Russ said.

He showed us an example of a quick-change costume. It looked just like a regular one, but there were hidden fasteners that made it easy to take off and put on.

So cool!

We did a few practice changes for Felicia. Getting her into and out of her costumes was harder than I thought, especially doing it as quickly as Felicia demanded. It started to feel like we were a pit crew changing tires during a race. (See?! I knew quick changes had something to do with cars.)

My favorite outfit was this big, poufy dress with a tearaway skirt. (Or at least I **thought** it was a tearaway skirt. . . .)

GET ME OUT OF THIS THING! MY BIG MOMENT IS NEXT!

I GOT IT!

WAIT, BABYMOUSE—

YANK!

RIIPPP!!!

THAT'S THE DRESS WITH THE VELCRO SKIRT.

TALK ABOUT "TEARING IT UP," BABYMOUSE.

GRUMBLE.

Waiting to Rehearse

Finally, the day of the dress rehearsal arrived! All of us gathered in a classroom.

"Circle up, everyone," Mr. Russ said. "Time for a last-minute chat."

We formed a big circle, which was kind of difficult because there were so many of us, and lots of people were already in costume.

"As we do this run-through," Mr. Russ said, "it's important to keep **one** thing in mind at all times. This is a collaborative effort. Things will go wrong. It's up to you to be willing to pitch in and problem-solve. There is no ego in theater. We worked hard. Now let's show them what we got!"

Everyone nodded.

We all put our hands into the middle of the circle.

"Showtime on three," Raj said. "One, two, three!"

The cast and crew sprang into action.

Millie and I had our work cut out for us with the quick costume changes. I was starting to feel a little nervous, but I reminded myself this was totally normal.

Besides, I'd gotten in lots of quick-change practice before bed last night.

But even with the flurry of initial excitement, often I was just left hanging out backstage. I was starting to realize being

part of a play meant a lot of doing nothing—
followed by stressful bursts of action and
chaos, of course.

Raj walked up to me.

"Want to see something cool?" he asked.

"Sure!" I replied. "I don't have to help
Felicia change anymore tonight."

"Great," Raj replied. "Follow me."

He led me through a secret door, up some
stairs, and all the way to a narrow plank
above the stage.

"The catwalk is my favorite place," Raj told me.

"Why do they call it a catwalk?" I asked, looking around for some kittens.

"I have no idea!" Raj replied. "There are lots of funny words for things in theater."

"Really?" I asked. "Like what?"

Raj pointed to the front of the stage, near the audience. "Do you know what that's called?"

"Of course!" I replied. "The stage."

Raj laughed. "Actually, it's the apron."

We sat on the catwalk, watching the play unfold below.

"It's the final scene," Raj whispered.

I smiled and felt some butterflies in my chest. I wasn't sure if it was because we were so high up, or because of what was about to happen. The final scene was when Felicia's and Georgie's characters shared a kiss. I was still kind of shocked by the whole kiss thing, to be honest.

"I can't believe they're going to kiss!" I told Raj.

Raj laughed.

"They won't really kiss," he explained. "Felicia just holds up her parasol, and they both lean behind it and **pretend** to kiss. Classic theater illusion."

"Oh wow!" I said. "I wish there was a trick like that for doing homework!"

Raj laughed so hard, he had to cover his mouth to keep from being too loud.

"Me too!" he replied.

Jitters

It was the evening before opening night. I was sitting at the dinner table with my family.

"Would you like some peas, Babymouse?" Dad asked me.

"I prefer artichokes," I said, practicing my line.

"What?" Dad asked. "I thought you hated artichokes."

"I do," I said, nodding, "but I **prefer** them."

Mom smiled. "Sounds like someone is ready for the big show tomorrow," she said.

"Yep," I replied.

"I've invited the extended family to see the show," she said.

My stomach dropped. "Who?"

"So far on my list of people who can come, there's Grampamouse; all our aunts, uncles, cousins, and cousins twice removed; your old babysitters; and Miss Dotty."

"Isn't that the lady who accidentally wandered into our last family reunion?" Dad asked.

"Yes," Mom confirmed. "We're not related. But she's been sending us holiday cards ever since, so she's pretty much family."

I gulped and felt a tingle of unease.

Mom kept talking. "How thrilling! So many people are coming to see **you**, Babymouse!"

But I wasn't thrilled. In fact, I was nervous. Really, really nervous. My stomach was doing backflips.

My mom looked at me. "What's wrong, Babymouse?"

"I don't know about all these people coming to see me," I said.

She gave me an understanding look. "Ah, I see. You have a case of the jitters."

"Jitters?"

"Stage fright," my mom clarified. "It's perfectly natural. I remember feeling the same way when I had my first ballet recital."

It didn't feel perfectly natural. It felt terrifying. These people were going to be watching **me.** What if I messed up? What if I missed my cue? What if I forgot my lines?

(I mean my **line.**)

All of a sudden, I wasn't very hungry anymore.

"May I be excused, please?" I asked.

"Sure, Babymouse," my mom said. "All you need is a good night's sleep."

"And don't say 'Macbeth,'" my dad added cryptically.

I looked at him. "Huh?"

"**Macbeth** is a play by Shakespeare. It's considered very bad luck for an actor to say 'Macbeth' in a theater. Instead, you're supposed to say 'the Scottish play.'"

"What happens if I say 'Macbeth'?" I asked.

"The play will be cursed." Dad shrugged. "Or you'll have a mysterious death."

HERE LIES
BABYMOUSE.

SHE ATE
THE HOT LUNCH.

My mouth dropped open.

Then my dad snapped his fingers. "Now I

remember. There's an antidote. If you say it, just run outside and spit three times."

All I could do was stare at him.

"Ignore your father," my mother said. "They're just silly superstitions."

Of course, I couldn't ignore what he'd said. I only ignored things my parents told me to pay attention to.

So I dove straight down the rabbit hole of the internet. After spending an hour on my computer, I learned there are a lot of superstitions when it comes to theater. One is that if you have a bad dress rehearsal, you'll have a good opening night. Seeing as the fog machine had exploded during rehearsal yesterday and we'd had to call the fire department, I figured we'd be in for a great opening night. So . . . yay?

But most of the superstitions are downright strange. And if you break any of the rules, you'll have bad luck.

I guess it was lucky my costume wasn't blue.

Just terrifying.

☆ ♡ ☆

After I got into my pajamas, I tucked my script under my pillow. This was supposed to be good luck for an actor. Also, I was hoping it would help me remember my line.

When I fell asleep, I dreamed it was opening night. The audience filled the seats. The curtains rose. Then I heard my cue.

Opening Night

The big night had finally arrived. A huge banner announced it to the school.

There was a flurry of activity around me backstage.

Mr. Russ kept everything moving, Raj did a couple of last-minute set fixes, and Felicia barked orders to the cast and crew.

"Twenty minutes to get in costume and makeup before the curtain goes up," Mr. Russ announced.

"Eep!" I squealed.

I quickly wiggled into my clown outfit and big, floppy shoes. I sat down at the vanity to put on my makeup. I had decided to do it myself. But my hands were shaking from being so nervous, and I accidentally dropped a dark-red lipstick on the white part of my costume.

I felt like I was going to scream or cry or throw up or all those things at once. But Millie swooped in and came to the rescue. She used white shoe polish to cover up the mess.

"The show must go on!" she said with a smile.

Raj popped his head into the makeup room. "Places, everyone," he said.

He waved to me. "Break a leg, Babymouse," he said with a grin before disappearing out the door.

Millie and I took three deep breaths together. It helped me calm down . . . a little. I breathed out the last big breath as the curtain went up.

We made it halfway through the show without any mistakes. I couldn't believe it!

During intermission, I peeked through the curtain to see the rows and rows of seats taken up by my family.

The house lights dimmed, and the show was back on. I listened closely. The time had arrived for me to say my line. My heart was pounding in my chest.

I heard my cue: "If only a clown were here!"

I rushed out onto the stage, ready to nail my line. But when I got there, the bright lights made me freeze. I wondered if anyone would be able to hear me over the pounding in my chest.

You can do it, Babymouse, I told myself. **You can prefer artichokes.**

I gathered up my courage. My brows furrowed. My jaw set. My eyes narrowed. With the intensity of a million Babymouses, I said the line. . . .

PEAS ARE TASTY, BUT I PREFER ARTICHOKES.

"**Brava!**" Miss Dotty yelled from the audience.

I smiled as I walked off the set. Millie was waiting for me backstage.

"How did I do?" I asked nervously.

I could tell by her expression that "great" was not the first word coming to mind.

"Well, you were, um, very **dramatic**, Babymouse," she said finally.

Quick Change

The craziness of the play continued. I scurried around backstage, helping Felicia with her costume changes. During one of them, Felicia couldn't find her shoe. She started flipping out.

"I need a shoe right **now**," she growled.
So I did the only thing I could think of. . . .

TALK ABOUT A CARNIVAL.

☆ ♡ ☆

The hallways were crowded with actors and people moving sets.

"I'm going for a walk," Felicia announced.

"Do you think that's a good idea?" I asked. "It's almost time for your big scene!"

She gave me a nasty look. My face went as red as when I had the allergic reaction.

Georgie cut in. "I'll go with you, Felicia," he said. "We'll both keep an eye on the time."

I shrugged and went to make sure the parasol was ready for the final scene.

Millie ran up to me, carrying the last change of costumes.

"I can't find Felicia or Georgie!" she exclaimed.

"What do you mean?" I asked.

"No one can find them!" she said. "They've disappeared!"

I began to panic, too.

"They said they were going for a walk," I told her. "But they could be anywhere by now."

"It's the final scene!" she replied.

"We have to do something!" I agreed.

Suddenly, I remembered what Raj had told me on the catwalk.

CLASSIC THEATER ILLUSION.

ILLUSION. ILLUSION. ILLUSION. ILLUSION. ILLUSION. ILLUSION. ILLUSION. ILLUSION.

"The show must go on!" I reminded Millie.

I tried to think fast. "If we put on the main characters' costumes and pose behind the parasol when the scene changes, maybe—just maybe—no one will notice it's us instead of Felicia and Georgie."

Millie's eyes widened.

"That could work," she said. "But neither of us is tall enough to look like Georgie."

"Leave that to me!" I replied.

I rummaged through my backpack and pulled out the lost polka-dot sock.

Then I popped my head into the custodian's closet to grab the hose from his vacuum cleaner.

Of course, he freaked out when he saw me again. . . .

169

The lights came up. The music swelled.
Millie and I were ready for action.

Curtain Call

Finally, the show was over. I took a bow with a smile that felt as wide as the stage itself.

After the show, my family waited for me by the back exit. Mom handed me a big bouquet. I laughed when I saw that instead of flowers, they had given me a bunch of artichokes.

"It was my idea!" Squeak said proudly.

"You were wonderful, Babymouse!" Mom said, grinning from ear to ear. "So much talent packed into one fabulous line."

"That wasn't my only big scene," I said with a smile.

I told them about Millie and me secretly acting out the final scene.

"Well done, Babymouse!" Dad exclaimed.

My heart was beating fast again, but this time because I was so happy and excited. I really felt like a star!

After what felt like a million pictures with every person in my family (including one that Miss Dotty said she'd use for next year's holiday card!), Mom and Dad took Squeak home, and I headed backstage.

The whole cast and crew were meeting there for a big wrap party. We were all tired and sore from working so hard.

"We did it!" Raj exclaimed. Everyone hugged and high-fived. It felt great to be part of a team.

I thought back on the whole experience. It wasn't what I'd expected—the hard work, the fear, the stress—but it was **worth** it!

Eventually, the excitement gave way to exhaustion. I collapsed into a chair.

"I could sleep for a week!" I exclaimed.

"That will have to wait, Babymouse," Mr. Russ said. "I'll see you all tomorrow morning at eight to strike the stage."

Huh? I thought. **That's weird.**

"What does that mean?" I whispered to Raj. "Why would we **hit** the stage?"

YEAH! WHY WOULD YOU HIT ME?

Raj laughed.

"Striking the stage means to take every-thing down and clean up."

"Everything?" I asked.

"Everything," he repeated.

UGH.

YOU WILL LOVE YOUR CREWMATES EVEN MORE AT EIGHT A.M., BABYMOUSE.

The next day, I dragged myself out of bed bright and early to help strike the stage with my friends. Luckily, demolishing the set was almost as much fun as putting it together.

I UNSCREWED.

I UNDRILLED.

I EVEN UN-**WHATEVER-THIS-THING-IS**-ED!

When everything was taken apart and cleaned up, we sat around and had bagels and orange juice.

"Where's Felicia?" I asked, wiping cream cheese off my face. "I haven't seen her since she disappeared last night."

Georgie grinned.

"Well, after we got stuck outside, she tried to climb back in through a window, and fell into the dumpster."

"No way!" I replied.

"Yeah, and it gets worse!" he added. "Inside the dumpster was a skunk, and he wasn't too happy about having a visitor."

COUNTY WASTE

I covered my mouth in disbelief.

We all tried not to laugh, but it was obvious that everyone thought this was pretty funny (even Melinda and Berry).

Raj came over and sat next to me. He was holding a big rolled-up canvas.

"Hey, Babymouse," he said. "Can I keep this as a souvenir?"

He unrolled the canvas to show my painting of the sunset.

"It would look cool in the Audiovisual room," he added quickly.

"You want **that**?" I asked.

"Definitely," he replied.

"Sure."

Suddenly, there was a loud noise. Millie excitedly burst through the door.

"Extra! Extra!" she yelled. "Hot off the presses!"

She held up a review from the local paper.

CARNIVAL CHAOS! END SCENE

ACT III, Scene 5

A bucolic park. The sun is setting. We see the carnival in the background. Clarabelle enters the park, looking sad.

CLARABELLE

Maybe I should give up the carnival life?
Is it worth losing my one chance at love?

Fred enters the park.

FRED

Clarabelle!

Clarabelle is startled.

CLARABELLE

Fred?

FRED

You don't have to give up the carnival! I'll join it.
Can you use another strong man?

CLARABELLE
(tearful)
You'll always be my strong man.

Clarabelle runs over to Fred. They embrace.

FRED

I love you!

CLARABELLE

I love you, too, Fred. You are worth more than
cotton candy or a goldfish in a bowl.

Fred and Clarabelle kiss behind her parasol.

The sun goes down. We see the carnival still lit up.

Blackout. Curtain.

BABYMOUSE + LOCKER VERSION!

CARNIVAL CHAOS! END SCENE

ACT III, Scene 5

A bucolic park. The sun is setting. We see the carnival in the background. Clarabelle enters the park, looking sad.

CLARABELLE
Maybe I should give up the carnival life?
Is it worth losing my one chance at love?

~~CLOWN #1~~ Fred enters the park.

CLOWN #1
~~FRED~~
~~Clarabelle!~~ CRASH!

Clarabelle is startled.

CLARABELLE
~~Fred?~~ CLOWN #1?

CLOWN #2 ~~FRED~~
~~You don't have to give up the carnival! I'll join it.~~
~~Can you use another strong man?~~

Did someone ask for a clown?

CLARABELLE
~~(tearful)~~
You'll always be my ~~strong man.~~ Clown #2.

Clarabelle runs over to ~~Fred. They embrace.~~ the Clowns.

CLOWN #2 ~~FRED~~
Let's dance! ~~I love you!~~

~~CLARABELLE~~
~~I love you, too, Fred. You are worth more than~~
~~cotton candy or a goldfish in a bowl.~~

~~Fred and Clarabelle kiss behind her parasol.~~

The sun goes down. We see the carnival still lit up.

Blackout. Curtain.

They break-dance and go back to the carnival. THE END!

☆ ♥ ☆

About the Authors

Jennifer L. Holm and **Matthew Holm** are a **New York Times** bestselling sister-and-brother team. They are the creators behind several popular series: Babymouse, Squish, The Evil Princess vs. the Brave Knight, and My First Comics. The Eisner Award–winning Babymouse books have introduced millions of children to graphic novels. Jennifer is also the **New York Times** bestselling author of **The Fourteenth Goldfish** and several other highly acclaimed novels, including three Newbery Honor winners: **Our Only May Amelia, Penny from Heaven,** and **Turtle in Paradise.** Matthew is also the author of **Marvin and the Moths** with Jonathan Follett.

HAVE YOU READ THE *EPIC* FIRST BOOK IN THE SERIES?
TURN THE PAGE FOR A SNEAK PEEK!

New York Times bestselling authors of *Sunny Side Up*

JENNIFER L. HOLM & MATTHEW HOLM

BABYMOUSE
TALES FROM THE LOCKER

Lights, Camera, Middle School!

Monster Movie

Middle school was like a movie.

Not a romantic-smoochy movie or a swashbuckling-pirate movie. Or even a space-aliens-invade-the-world kind of movie.

It was a **monster movie**.

The hallways were crawling with spooky creatures.

You were always having to run for your life.

And everywhere you turned, someone was trying to eat your brains.

But sometimes the scariest thing about middle school involved **whiskers**.

And, believe me, I know whiskers.

My name is Babymouse.

And this is my Tale from the Locker.

I was standing in front of my locker, trying to open it. As usual, the door was stuck. I had a love-hate relationship with my locker, aka "Locker." Mostly I hated the big metal bully. (I swear it ate my homework!)

I banged on it for a minute, and finally it popped open.

"Hey, Babymouse," a voice called.

I turned around to see Felicia Furrypaws.

If this was a monster movie, Felicia would be a Zombie. At middle school, Zombies travelled in packs and dressed the same. Instead of hunting brains, they wanted **stuff**: whatever was cool and "in." It could be wedge sandals or ruffled scarves or sparkly lip gloss. They just **had** to have it.

GLURG!
MOOAAAN!!
BRAANOS!
STUUUFFFFFFFF!!!!!
BRAANODS!!
COOOOLL!!!
SHUFFLE   STAGGER

Felicia and I had gone to elementary school together. With her perfectly straight whiskers, she had always been one of the popular girls. Today, she was sporting a plaid skirt, white tights, and a crisp white shirt with a ruffled bow. She looked stylish and French, like she'd walked out of a fashion ad. Her look shouted "Cool Girl."

And my look? I wasn't quite sure. I definitely wanted my look to say:

I'M SWEET!

I'M SENSITIVE!

I'M CLEVER!

FWIP!

ZAP!

I'M DARING!

But I also wanted my look to say a lot of other things, including:

I LOVE BOOKS!

I THINK KOALA BEARS ARE UNDERAPPRECIATED!

KNOCK KNOCK!

I KNOW A LOT OF KNOCK-KNOCK JOKES!

NO MORE!

I'M A GOOD CONVERSATIONALIST!

I KNOW THREE FRENCH WORDS!

C'EST LA VIE.

It was kind of hard to translate all this into a "look."

Speaking of looks, Felicia was staring at my face.

"Did you straighten your whiskers?" she asked.

"Yes!" I said with a bright smile.

It was technically true. My whiskers were straight, even if they weren't exactly mine. See, I'd tried straightening my whiskers using a fancy cream, but the harsh chemicals had burned them right off. So this morning, I'd glued on some false whiskers to hide the damage.

"You might want to use more glue next time," she told me.

"What do you mean?" I asked.

"That," she said, pointing at my nose. I realized that one of my whiskers was ... dangling?

She blew at it.

I watched in horror as it fell off and floated to the floor in slow motion.

Felicia walked off, laughing.

Le sigh.

I was never going to be famous for my whiskers.

New York Times bestselling authors of *Sunny Side Up*

JENNIFER L. HOLM & MATTHEW HOLM

BABYMOUSE
TALES FROM THE LOCKER

Miss Communication

Babymouse has a smartphone, and she's not afraid to use it!

WATCH OUT, BIG CITY. . . .
BABYMOUSE IS ABOUT TO HIT THE TOWN!

New York Times bestselling authors of *Sunny Side Up*
JENNIFER L. HOLM & MATTHEW HOLM

BABYMOUSE
TALES FROM THE LOCKER

School-Tripped

Will a class field trip with **no chaperones** be as thrilling as
Babymouse thinks? Or will life in the Big City trip her up big-time?